Garfield's PET FORCE™

THE OUTRAGEOUS ORIGIN

Garfield's PET FORCE™

THE OUTRAGEOUS ORIGIN

Created by
Jim Davis

Character development by
Mark Acey & Gary Barker

Written by
Michael Teitelbaum

Illustrated by
Gary Barker & Larry Fentz

Produced by Creative Media Applications, Inc. and Paws Inc.

Graphics by Jeff Wesley

This edition published in 2001.

Copyright © 1997 by Paws Incorporated. All rights reserved.
Pet Force™ is a registered trademark of Paws Incorporated.

Published by Troll Communications L.L.C.

ISBN 0-8167-7206-1

Printed in Canada.

10 9 8 7 6 5 4 3 2 1

Introduction

When a group of lovable pets — Garfield, Odie, Arlene, Nermal, and Pooky — are transported to an alternate universe, they become a mighty superhero team known as . . . *Pet Force!*

Garzooka — Large and in charge, he is the fearless and famished leader of Pet Force. He's a ferocious feline with nerves of steel, a razor-sharp right claw, and the awesome ability to fire gamma-radiated hairballs (as well as deadly one-liners) from his mouth.

Odious — Although he is utterly clueless, he possesses great strength, ultra-slippery slobber, and a super-stretchy stun tongue. One zap of his lethal wet tongue causes a total mental meltdown in anyone he unleashes it upon.

Starlena — She sings a *purrfectly* pitched siren song ("the meow that wows!"). Anyone who hears her hypnotic song immediately falls into a trance — except Garzooka.

Abnermal — He has a body temperature of absolute zero; one touch of his icy paw freezes foes in their tracks. He can extend a nuke-proof force field to protect himself, as well as the other members of Pet Force. His pester-power — more annoying than your little brother! — is one power Garzooka could live without.

Compooky — Part-computer, part-teddy, this cyberbear extraordinaire is not only incredibly cute, but is also the mental giant of the team (not that big a deal).

Behold the mighty Pet Force! *Let the fur fly!*

Garfield's PET FORCE™

THE OUTRAGEOUS ORIGIN

1

The sleek rectangular spaceship, the *Lightspeed Lasagna*, silently sliced through the vast void of space. Not the space that *you* see when you look up at the starry sky at night. This space, these stars, were in a parallel universe — a universe similar to, but not the same as, our own.

On board the *Lightspeed Lasagna*, the five super-powered beings known as Pet Force were tracking their enemy, the evil veterinarian Vetvix. Garzooka, leader of Pet Force, scanned the glowing instrument panel before him.

"No sign of furtron particles in this sector," announced Garzooka. He shifted his heavily muscled body in his seat. His bulging biceps rippled under his skintight costume. His round jaw was clenched firmly, his expression permanently serious. His cape was bunched up behind him. He shifted his weight and pulled it out.

Compooky — a half-teddy bear, half-computer of tremendous intelligence — beeped and buzzed, then he spoke. "I am certain from my star field analysis that Vetvix's *Orbiting Clinic of Chaos* is nearby," he reported.

"And we know that her *Clinic* emits furtron particles," purred Starlena. "Something is not right here."

At the mention of furtron particles, Odious, the strongest member of Pet Force, got very excited. His super-slippery slobber splattered everywhere. He picked up something from the floor and trotted over to Garzooka. His massive chest cast a shadow across the Pet Force leader as he handed him what he had found. Odious nodded and pointed to the object that Garzooka now held in his hand.

Garzooka sighed deeply. "That's not a furtron particle, Odious," he explained. "It's a hairball I coughed up this morning." Among Garzooka's superpowers was the ability to fire gamma-radiated hairballs from his mouth. Fortunately for Odious, the hairball he had picked up was of the more normal, less deadly variety.

"Garzooka! I've got something!" shouted Abnermal as his fingers flew furiously over his computer keyboard. Shimmering blue waves filled his monitor. Abnermal analyzed the energy readings on his screen, then announced his astonishing discovery. "A cloaking mechanism," he said. "Vetvix is using some type of cloaking mechanism."

"But her *Orbiting Clinic of Chaos* is much too

big to cloak," replied a puzzled Garzooka. "It would be impossible!"

"She is not cloaking the station," explained Compooky, quickly scanning Abnermal's findings. "She is simply cloaking the furtron particles."

"She's as clever as she is evil," snarled Garzooka through clenched teeth.

"Yes," agreed Starlena. "And she's as evil as she is brilliant."

"True," added Abnermal. "And she's as brilliant as she is devious."

"Affirmative," Compooky joined in. "My analysis indicates that she is as devious as she is powerful!"

All eyes turned to Odious. He smiled, nodded, and drooled. No one was surprised.

"I have adjusted our sensors to defeat the cloak," said Compooky. "The image should be coming on-screen now."

Suddenly thousands of furtron particles appeared on Garzooka's monitor. "Nice work, Compooky and Abnermal. We've picked up the villain's foul stench. Now all we have to do is follow it right to her *Orbiting Clinic of Chaos*. Odious, full speed!"

Odious dashed off toward the back of the *Lightspeed Lasagna* at full speed. Slipping and sliding on his own slobber, he finally crashed into the rear wall of the ship. "I meant full speed for the *ship*, Odious — not for you," Garzooka explained. Then he reached over and pressed a control switch on Odious's instrument panel. The deafening sound of proton-powered engines filled the ship. In a burst of crimson and orange flame, the *Lightspeed Lasagna* zoomed off at top speed.

As Pet Force followed the trail of now-exposed furtron particles toward the *Orbiting Clinic of Chaos*, Garzooka's thoughts turned to Vetvix's reign of terror over the innocent pets of this universe. "She must be stopped," he muttered softly.

In her Lethal Lab on board the *Orbiting Clinic of Chaos*, Vetvix had invented a molecular scrambling ray, which was powered by her dark magic. She kidnapped animals from all over the universe and used her ray to mutate them into strange and terrifying creatures — such as a half-gorilla, half-pit bull; a half-lion, half-alligator; and other half-crazed combinations. Vetvix controlled these fierce creations with her powerful telepathic abilities, using the creatures to make the peace-loving pets on the planets throughout the galaxy into slaves. All this was part of her master plan to rule the universe!

Garzooka was shaken out of his deep thoughts by the urgent whistling of Compooky. "Vetvix's *Orbiting Clinic of Chaos* is on-screen now!" said the supercomputer. There, filling his monitor screen, Garzooka saw something that made him gasp. His big eyes narrowed as he drew a short breath and stared at the most humongous space

station he had ever encountered in all his years of cruising the cosmos.

The *Orbiting Clinic of Chaos* loomed before them. Light from a nearby star reflected off its glass-and-steel outer shell. It hovered like a giant office building out in space — a huge rectangular factory of fear.

Suddenly one of the *Clinic*'s many thousands of windows opened and a laser weapon fired at the *Lightspeed Lasagna*. Its powerful blast scorched the ship.

"Well, there's a nice, friendly 'hello' from the Vetvix Welcoming Committee," said Starlena. "What's next? A fruit basket and some sponge cake?"

"A hull stress analysis indicates that the next laser blast will destroy the spaceship," Compooky reported calmly.

"We won't need to worry if we're quick enough," said Garzooka. "Everybody strap in. We're about to dock on the *Orbiting Clinic of Chaos*!"

Garzooka skillfully piloted the *Lightspeed Lasagna* into one of the *Clinic*'s open docking bays. When the ship was securely docked, Pet Force sprang into action.

"Now let's show Vetvix what we're made of," said Garzooka, leading the others from the ship. *"Let the fur fly!"*

The Pet Force leader extended his right arm and spread his fingers wide. Out popped his razor-sharp claw. Garzooka's claw glinted in the ship's exterior lights as he ripped a gash in the solid iron door leading into the *Clinic*. The opening was big enough for the superpowered friends to slip inside. Compooky remained behind with the ship, ready in case a quick getaway was needed.

Pet Force was immediately met by a squadron of Vetvix's molecularly scrambled animals. Garzooka fired a series of gamma-radiated hairballs, which took out a group of the mutant beasts. Abnermal used his freeze-touch power to stop several more in their tracks. Odious lashed out with his super-stretchy stun tongue, scrambling the brains of each animal he struck.

The first wave of opposition was wiped out. Pet Force now moved deeper into the *Clinic*. "We've got to make it to Vetvix's Lethal Lab, the heart of her operation," announced Garzooka. "But how do we find it?"

Starlena pointed to a sign on the wall that read:
ELEVATORS OF EVIL TO LETHAL LAB.
VISITS BY APPOINTMENT ONLY.

"To the Elevators of Evil!" shouted Garzooka.

The heroes dashed down the hallway, only to run into a second wave of mutated menaces. Starlena took a deep breath, then sang out loudly with her hypnotic song. The scrambled creatures stumbled aimlessly in trances. Abnermal covered his ears so as not to be affected. Garzooka was the only being immune to Starlena's song. Odious was in his own trance most of the time anyway, so it was hard to tell whether or not he was affected.

Having disposed of this second group of foes, Pet Force stepped into the Elevators of Evil. Garzooka pressed the button labeled LETHAL LAB, 485TH FLOOR. Suddenly the elevator filled with the sound of cruel laughter.

"It's a trap!" shouted Starlena.

"So nice of you to follow my signs, Pet Fools!" snarled Vetvix. Her voice came from a speaker in the ceiling of the elevator car. "Only you didn't read the sign carefully enough. It said 'Visits by appointment only.' And you don't have an appointment! There's a penalty for that — and you, Pet Fools, will pay with your lives!"

Before anyone in the elevator could move, the small car was flooded with a powerful beam of light from Vetvix's molecular scrambling ray. It bathed the members of Pet Force in its deadly energy.

Could this be the end of Pet Force?

Will our heroes be scrambled and fused into some hideous four-headed, eight-armed, eight-legged creature totally under Vetvix's control?

Is there no escape?

Be sure to pick up the next issue of *Pet Force*!

2

Our Universe, Jon's Backyard . . .

Nermal put down the *Pet Force* comic book he
had been holding firmly in his paws. "Wow!"
he exclaimed. "What a cool story! What an incredibly exciting adventure! I can't wait for the next
issue to see how they get out of that elevator!"

Garfield and his friends — Nermal, Arlene,
Odie, and Pooky — were in the middle of a backyard barbecue. Jon Arbuckle — Garfield and
Odie's nerdy owner — stood at the barbecue grill,
flipping burgers and hot dogs. Arlene sat next to
Nermal, helping him with the hard words in the
comic book. Odie pranced up and down in front of
a hedge of Jon's favorite rosebushes, slobbering
on the beautiful pink flowers. And Garfield, with
Pooky by his side, had positioned himself as close
to the grill as possible without becoming a part of
lunch himself. He wanted to be first in line for each
new round of barbecue goodies.

Nermal dashed over to Garfield, still bursting with excitement from what he had just read. "Hey, look at this, Garfield!" he screeched in a high-pitched, ultra-annoying voice. "Check out this double-page splash panel. Look! Look! The *Pet Force* guys are in this elevator, only the elevator is really a trap set by Vetvix. She turns on her molecular scrambling ray and *ZAP!* They're all going to be rearranged and scrambled together, with their arms and legs and heads stuck on the wrong bodies, and — oh, you know what's cool? This is issue number ninety-nine of *Pet Force.* Next issue is going to be the giant, double-sized, super-spectacular anniversary issue with an embossed, gold foil, three-D, holographic, glow-in-the-dark cover! Cool, huh?"

Throughout Nermal's entire explosion of enthusiasm, Garfield sat stuffing hot dogs into his face. He listened to the younger cat halfheartedly, keeping one ear peeled for Jon's voice saying, "Get a hot dog. Get it while it's a *hot* dog!" Each time he said it, Jon giggled at his own little joke. A very little joke, in Garfield's opinion.

"I can't figure out what you see in comic books, Nermal," said Garfield, in between bites of his hot dog.

"Well, you see pictures and words and sound effects — and ads for toys," explained Nermal.

Garfield gave Nermal one of his *What am I, as dumb as Jon?* looks. "I *mean*, I just don't understand what good comic books are," Garfield said. "You can't eat them, and they're too small to use as blankets." Garfield took the comic from Nermal and flipped through a few pages. "Besides," he continued, "this stuff is totally impossible. Super-powered beings flying around in a spaceship battling evil veterinarians? I mean, come on! Of course, the biggest flaw with this comic book is that it's not about me." He popped another hot dog into his mouth.

"Do you think you could leave a hot dog or two for anyone else, Garfield?" asked Arlene.

I doubt it! thought Garfield, as he shoved another two into his mouth at the same time.

"Or are you working up your strength for that big nap you intend to take later?" Arlene continued.

"Your meager insults simply bounce right off me, Arlene," Garfield replied, smirking.

"That's no shock," said Arlene. "Everything bounces off that fat frame of yours!"

While Arlene and Garfield continued to trade put-downs, Odie came trotting over. He happily slobbered all over the comic book that sat open on the ground next to Garfield.

"Odie!" shouted Nermal. "Be careful. I'm saving this comic book. I'm a collector, you know."

"Yeah, a collector of dust," Garfield mumbled between bites.

"I have the first ninety-eight issues of *Pet Force*

carefully preserved in sealed plastic bags," explained Nermal. "Now that I've read it, this one's getting sealed up, too."

Odie nodded furiously, his tongue flopping wildly, sending slobber everywhere.

"I can't wait for issue number one hundred!" exclaimed Nermal excitedly, holding the comic book behind his back to protect it from further doggie drool. "It's going to be the giant, double-sized, super-spectacular anniversary issue with an embossed, gold foil, three-D, holographic, glow-in-the-dark cover!"

"We've heard," said Garfield in the same bored voice he used when discussing anything other than food or naps.

Jon loyally manned his post at the grill, dressed in a striped shirt, checkered slacks, and a pair of white vinyl shoes. He looked like something that might show up in a golfer's nightmare after eating some week-old chili just before bedtime. Over his stunningly hideous outfit, Jon wore an apron that said HAVIN' A HECKUVA BAR-B-Q!

Looking up from the dozens of hot dogs he was still cooking on the grill — all of which were being eaten by Garfield — Jon noticed Nermal's *Pet Force* comic. "Is that a comic book you've got there?" he asked.

No, thought Garfield. *It's a twelve-volume encyclopedia.*

"I read lots of comic books when I was a kid,"

said Jon, his mind drifting back to his youth. *"Armadillo Man Versus the Moon Monsters from Mars, Captain Cosmic and His Radiation Rangers, The Masked Turkey on the Planet of the Living Rocks.* Great stuff! Classics, all! Boy, I loved reading those comic books. I think you can learn a lot from comics. I know I did."

Like what? thought Garfield. *How to dress like a total geek-a-saurus?*

Jon had become so absorbed in his thoughts about his comic-book-reading youth that he had forgotten to keep an eye on the grill. The next hot dog he handed Garfield looked like a long piece of coal.

"I, for one, think comic books are wonderful," said Arlene. "They introduce youngsters like Nermal to both reading and art. Plus, they stir the imagination."

"I'd much rather stir a nice spaghetti sauce," replied Garfield. "Besides, comics are just total nonsense. None of this *Pet Force* stuff could possibly be true."

3

The story so far . . .

As it turned out, Garfield couldn't have been more wrong. Not only *could* Pet Force exist, it *did* exist — but not in the universe you and Garfield call home. What the fat cat didn't realize was that our universe — the one filled with trees and buildings, and pets and food, and Garfield, Odie, Arlene, Nermal, Pooky, and Jon — was only one of millions of universes that exist parallel to our own.

It was in one of these parallel universes that Pet Force actually did exist.

This alternate universe was ruled by the wise and kind Emperor Jon, who looked a lot like the Jon we know and love in our universe, except that Emperor Jon dressed a heck of a lot better. You know, flowing robes, gold crown, striped shirt, and checkered slacks — well, some things are the same in all universes.

Emperor Jon lived on the planet Polyester. For generations, Emperor Jon's universe had been guarded by Pet Force — superpowered beings who had kept peace and justice in the universe for as long as anyone could remember. In recent times, the emperor's Pet Force had consisted of five incredibly powerful beings — Garzooka, Odious, Starlena, Abnermal, and Compooky. Ever since Jon became emperor, these five had fought for peace and freedom in the universe.

While Garfield, Odie, Arlene, Nermal, Pooky, and Jon were busy eating hot dogs and arguing about comic books at their backyard barbecue in *our* universe, trouble was brewing in Emperor Jon's universe — trouble in the form of an evil veterinarian named Vetvix, whose goal was total domination of that universe. Her skill in the ways of dark magic, coupled with her vast scientific and medical knowledge, made Vetvix a very real threat to peace and order in Emperor Jon's realm. The only thing that stood between Vetvix and her capture of the emperor's throne was the power of Pet Force!

4

Emperor Jon's universe . . .

The evil Vetvix strolled slowly down the corridor of her *Orbiting Clinic of Chaos*. Her bodysuit was covered with an animal paw-print pattern. Metal rings looped around her legs, waist, and arms. Her jet-black hair flowed down her back. On her forehead rested a large headband, in the center of which sat a power crystal — one of the many sources of her evil.

Her left hand firmly grasped a thick leather leash. The other end of the strap was attached to the sharply studded black-leather collar of her pet, Gorbull. Gorbull was the result of one of Vetvix's molecular experiments. His big hairy head was that of a gorilla. His dense muscular body was that of a pit bull. Gorbull was Vetvix's first combination creature, and for that reason he held a special place in her evil heart. While she sent many of her molecularly re-created animals

17

on dangerous missions, Gorbull became her prized pet.

"Here you go, poopsie," cooed Vetvix as she tossed a chunk of raw meat to Gorbull. The huge creature gobbled it down hungrily like a puppy snacking on a doggy treat, or Garfield snacking on almost anything. "Come. We have work to do before Pie-Rat joins us!"

Vetvix was awaiting the arrival of one of her henchmen, Space Pie-Rat, who was a huge rodent with a big appetite for food. Although Space Pie-Rat didn't know it at the moment, that appetite was about to get bigger — much bigger!

Vetvix and Gorbull wound their way through the twisting, turning hallways of the *Orbiting Clinic of Chaos*. The *Clinic* was the super-high-tech space station that served as Vetvix's headquarters, laboratory, and veterinary office. Deep in the heart of the *Clinic* sat Vetvix's Lethal Lab. This was her center of operations and the place where she carried out her ghoulish experiments. Test tubes filled with sickly green oozing liquids bubbled on top of open flames. Entering the lab, Gorbull trotted obediently over to the crate that served as his bed. He climbed in and began to gnaw on an old table leg that he used as his chew toy.

Meanwhile, Vetvix went to work putting the finishing touches on a levitation ray. The cannon-like device was an important part of her latest scheme to control the entire universe.

"Where is that reckless rodent?" snarled Vetvix as she made the final adjustments to her levitation ray. "He's always late, and he's always thinking with his stomach instead of his brain! Well, I might as well test this before he arrives."

Vetvix flipped on the power for her invention. A blue shaft of energy shot across the top of the machine. A few seconds later, a bright white beam spread forth from the device.

The levitation ray struck Gorbull's crate. The crate and Gorbull lifted high into the air. The usually fierce creature whimpered and peered out over the edge of the crate, which now hovered some fifteen feet off the ground. Gorbull looked down at the floor below and quickly ducked his head back in, hiding his eyes beneath his stubby round paws.

"It works!" cried Vetvix. "Now there is nothing to stop me!"

"Stop you from what?" said a voice behind her.

As Vetvix spun around to face the voice, she forgot that she was still holding the levitation ray. The beam swung with her and struck Space Pie-Rat, who stood in the entryway to the Lethal Lab cleaning his teeth with a toothpick.

Space Pie-Rat was a six-foot-tall rat. He wore a patch over his left eye and a red bandanna on his head, topped by a pirate hat. The levitation ray lifted the huge rodent into the air, while Gorbull's crate landed heavily on the floor. "Hey! What's going on?" shouted Pie-Rat. "I thought I was coming here to talk about a secret plan, not take a tour of your ceiling!"

"Ha ha ha!" chuckled Vetvix. "This *is* the secret plan, you fool. And don't tell me — you're late because you stopped off for a little something to eat on the way."

"I was hungry, Vetvix," whined Space Pie-Rat. "Give me a break!" Then he let out a huge burp. "'Scuse me. Can you put me down, please?"

"You are *always* hungry, Pie-Rat," said Vetvix. "But that is precisely why I chose you for this mission." Vetvix turned off the levitation ray. Space Pie-Rat landed on his feet.

"Now, what's this big, big mission you called me for?" asked Pie-Rat once he was standing safely on the ground.

"I'm going to ask you to think," began Vetvix. "So be careful. I don't want you to strain yourself. Tell me, Pie-Rat. What is the one thing that everyone needs?"

"A big-screen TV?" replied Pie-Rat.

"I knew this wasn't going to be easy," muttered Vetvix. "The answer is as plain as the mouth on your face. Food, you fool. Everyone, everywhere, needs food. Therefore, if I can control all the food in the universe, I can control the universe! And

that's where you and your enormous appetite come in."

"You want me to eat all the food in the universe?" asked Pie-Rat. "I don't know if even I could do that."

"I'm going to help you, my friend," cackled Vetvix. "First I will use my magic to cast a spell making your already huge appetite ten times bigger. Then you will go from planet to planet, eating all the food you can. Whatever you can't eat, you will steal with this levitation ray. I will supply you with huge cargo crafts, which will travel behind your ship. You'll be able to simply levitate entire warehouses full of food up to the waiting cargo ships. Soon, the starving planets of the universe will bow before the awesome power of Vetvix the Great!"

"Vetvix the Nut, if you ask me," whispered Pie-Rat under his breath.

"What was that?" shouted Vetvix.

"I — um, I said, 'When do we get started?'" replied Pie-Rat, nervous sweat pouring from beneath his bandanna.

"Right now," responded Vetvix. She closed her eyes, clenched her fists, and concentrated deeply. The power crystal on her headband began to glow with a bright red light, covering Space Pie-Rat. He felt himself grow hungrier and hungrier. Then suddenly the red light went off. The spell was complete.

"Wow!" exclaimed Pie-Rat. "I never thought I could be even hungrier than I usually am, but I'm *starving!*" He grabbed the table leg away from Gorbull. The annoyed pet growled as Pie-Rat bit off a chunk of wood and began to chew.

"Save your appetite, my feeble-minded friend," said Vetvix, smiling. "You've got a long mission ahead of you! Now gather an army of my most vicious mutant animal warriors and go. Go! Eat, my friend! Eat!"

As Space Pie-Rat raced from the Lethal Lab toward his docked ship, he could hear Vetvix's evil cackle echo throughout the entire *Orbiting Clinic of Chaos.*

5

Within days of Space Pie-Rat's meeting with Vetvix, word of food raids throughout the universe began to reach Emperor Jon. Strange reports of an enormous rodent leading an army of mutant animals on an eating rampage came in from all sectors.

In his palace on the planet Polyester, Emperor Jon shook his head in disbelief. He scanned a report telling of Space Pie-Rat and his army zooming from planet to planet in his spaceship, called the *Ravenous Rodent*, stealing all the food they could.

Emperor Jon paced back and forth in his throne room. The large room, centrally located in the palace, had seen its share of emperors over the centuries, but none was quite like Emperor Jon. The first thing Jon did when he took power was to redecorate so that the room more closely suited his personal taste and sense of style. The walls of the throne room were now covered from floor to ceiling with rec-room wooden paneling. The floor was made up of linoleum tiles set in a green-and-black-checkered pattern. They looked like they had been stolen from a school cafeteria.

Jon had replaced the emperor's hand-carved wooden throne — made centuries earlier from a single piece of oak by the finest craftspeople on the planet — with a vinyl-upholstered reclining lounge chair. "Stains wipe right off," Jon argued when his advisors cringed in horror at the change he had made.

A pair of large fuzzy dice hung off the back of the recliner. "I've got to get myself a car for those things one of these days," Jon said to himself, noticing the dice on one of his trips back and forth across the room. "Or at least a rearview mirror."

His easily distracted mind returned to the problem at hand. Emperor Jon knew what he had to do. He calmly walked from his throne over to the long banquet table located along one wall of the throne room.

He reached down and pressed a hidden button on one of the table legs. The enormous wooden tabletop began to rise, revealing row after row of computer control panels. The underside of the tabletop held a huge monitor screen, which now faced the emperor. He powered up the system, and a star field appeared on the monitor, stretching out into the black depths of infinite space.

I love that! Emperor Jon thought.

He flipped a series of switches on the control panel that loomed before him, sending out an emergency signal to Pet Force.

The star field that filled the monitor quickly faded. It was replaced by the image of Garzooka, leader of Pet Force.

"Emperor Jon," said Garzooka. "Since you've contacted me on the secret frequency that can be received only by Pet Force, I must assume that some horrible emergency threatens the very existence of our universe. And unless I miss my guess, Vetvix is somehow involved!"

"Your powers of deduction never cease to amaze me, Garzooka," replied Emperor Jon. "It is indeed Vetvix who threatens the universe once again. It seems she's been quite busy since you narrowly escaped from her elevator trap and her molecular scrambling ray. This time she's come up with a plan that involves her dark magic, her technological genius, and that miserable henchman of hers, Space Pie-Rat."

"Pie-Rat, huh?" growled Garzooka through clenched teeth. "I should have smelled that overgrown rodent all the way across the universe. What's that vermin up to now?"

Emperor Jon proceeded to fill Garzooka in on the details of Space Pie-Rat's food raids, his astounding eating binges, and the levitation of food supplies from numerous planets. "If Vetvix gets her hands on all the food in the universe, then my subjects will have to go to her in order to eat," said Emperor Jon, sounding very worried. "She would have absolute power over everyone."

"I understand, Emperor Jon," said Garzooka soberly. "Of course you can count on us!"

"I knew I could," replied the emperor. "The last report of a raid by Pie-Rat came from a planet near the Neutron Nebula. I suggest you start your search there. Good luck. Emperor Jon out."

Garzooka nodded at Emperor Jon's image on his view screen aboard the *Lightspeed Lasagna*. "Pet Force out," he said. Then he switched off his long-range communications system.

Garzooka turned to his teammates. "We have new orders, Pet Force," he announced. "Looks like our visit to the Pluto Pizza Parlor is going to have to wait. Too bad. I was looking forward to one of their Orion Onion and Martian Mushroom, triple-cheese, double-crust specials. But it seems that Space Pie-Rat has other plans for us."

"What's going on, Garzooka?" asked Starlena.

"Yeah, what's so important that we have to miss lunch?" added Abnermal. "I was really, really looking forward to that special pizza — those sweet onions, those mouthwatering mushrooms, gobs and gobs of the finest cheeses in the universe, all combined in a flavor medley guaranteed to —"

"We get the picture," interrupted Garzooka. "But I'm afraid that we've —"

"But what about the thick, tender crust and the

tangy sauce?" asked Abnermal, in a high, whiny voice. His pester-power was at full strength.

By this time Odious was standing in an ankle-deep pool of his own drool. Abnermal's description of the pizza they were about to miss had Odious's normally very active saliva glands working extra overtime. Slobber poured from his mouth like water from a fountain.

"Your pester-power is amazing, Abnermal," declared Garzooka. "But I'm afraid lunch will have to wait. Now, please mop up around Odious before he drowns while I explain our mission."

Abnermal reluctantly grabbed a mop as Garzooka told the others about Vetvix's plan to have Space Pie-Rat capture all the food in the universe. When he was finished, the members of Pet Force looked grim — except Odious, of course.

"Starlena, set course for the Neutron Nebula," ordered Garzooka.

Starlena called up the star charts for the region of space that contained the Neutron Nebula. She plotted a course from their current location, then fed it into the *Lightspeed Lasagna*'s computer.

"Compooky," continued Garzooka. "Can you give me the estimated travel time to the Nebula?"

Compooky buzzed and whistled as he did his calculation. "One hour, nine minutes," he replied.

Abnermal grunted as he wiped up the last bit of Odious's drool. "Not even enough time for an in-flight movie," he complained.

Exactly one hour and nine minutes later, Starlena's computer beeped.

"We're approaching the Neutron Nebula," she reported. "It should be fairly easy to find Pie-Rat's trail using our long-range rodent radar."

Before Garzooka had a chance to reply, the *Lightspeed Lasagna* was rocked by a laser blast that sent it spinning off course. "Looks like he found us first, Starlena," Garzooka grunted as he wrestled with the ship's controls. He managed to pull the ship out of its spin. "Have you found his exact position?"

"Got him!" replied Starlena. "Straight ahead."

As Garzooka gazed at his main view screen, the murky clouds of the Neutron Nebula appeared. There, on the edge of the nebula, he spotted the *Ravenous Rodent*. Space Pie-Rat's ship towed a long line of huge cargo vessels, like a locomotive engine pulling car after car of a freight train.

"Emperor Jon wasn't exaggerating," Starlena said. "It looks like Pie-Rat's got enough food there to feed all the planets in this entire region."

"Well, we're about to put a stop to all this madness," said Garzooka. "Full thrusters!"

The *Lightspeed Lasagna* shot forward like a bullet. Within seconds it was right on top of the *Ravenous Rodent*. To the great surprise of Pet Force, Space Pie-Rat abandoned his train of stolen food and took off at light speed, disappearing in a blinding flash of white. Pet Force followed.

Space Pie-Rat led them on a light-speed chase that took them halfway across the galaxy and back.

At last the *Lightspeed Lasagna* followed Pie-Rat out of light speed. The *Ravenous Rodent* seemed to be in trouble. Smoke poured from its rear end, and sparks flew out of its main engine.

"Looks like the *Rodent* made one too many light-speed jumps," said Garzooka with a satisfied smile. "We've got him. He's putting down on that small planet." Pet Force watched as Pie-Rat's ship spiraled toward a small, rocky planet below.

"We're going to land, too," ordered Garzooka.

The *Ravenous Rodent* continued its downward spiral and finally crashed onto the planet. The *Lightspeed Lasagna* set down not far from Pie-Rat's ship. "Stay alert, team," ordered Garzooka as Pet Force left their craft and explored the wreckage of the *Ravenous Rodent*.

"There are no life-forms aboard, Garzooka," announced Compooky after scanning the damaged vessel.

"So where's Pie-Rat?" asked Abnermal.

"There!" shouted Starlena, pointing to what looked like an abandoned structure not far from where they stood. "He must have crawled from his ship and hidden in that building."

The members of Pet Force carefully made their way to the building. It appeared to be an ancient factory, left to decay long ago by whoever had lived on this desolate planet. Stepping inside, they

saw broken windows and fallen ceilings, the ruins of a once-busy factory.

"No sign of Pie-Rat," said Garzooka, looking around.

"You're not looking in the right place," came a squeaky voice from above.

All five members of Pet Force looked up at once and saw Pie-Rat, apparently not injured at all, standing on a railing several floors above. Next to him stood Vetvix.

"So nice of you to follow Pie-Rat here," cackled Vetvix. "You saved me the trouble of mailing out invitations."

"So Pie-Rat's ship wasn't really in trouble," said Garzooka, sounding worried. "I think —"

His sentence was cut short as ten-inch-thick metal walls dropped down on all sides and on top of Pet Force.

"*It's a trap!*" all five shouted together.

6

Not losing a moment, the members of Pet Force each moved to a different section of the steel box that held them. Garzooka slashed at one wall with his razor-sharp claw, but even his steel talon and stupendous strength couldn't make a scratch in the glistening metal. The Pet Force leader next fired a series of gamma-radiated hairballs at the wall. Each one exploded in a blinding flash of gamma radiation upon impact, but when the smoke cleared, not a dent could be seen in the wall.

Starlena tried next. She let loose with her ear-piercing song, hoping the sonic vibrations would shatter their cage. The others all covered their ears so they wouldn't be affected by the sound. The sonic waves bounced harmlessly off the walls and ricocheted back, knocking Starlena off her feet. Garzooka rushed to her side.

"Are you all right?" he asked.

"I think so," she replied, shaking her head as she stood back up. "I've never had my siren song thrown back at me before. These walls must be made of some pretty serious stuff."

"Maybe I can lower the temperature of the metal enough to crack it," suggested Abnermal. He placed his paws flat on one of the walls and used his freeze power on the gleaming surface.

Ice spread out from Abnermal's paws, traveling along the wall in all directions. "This is as low as I can drop the temperature," said Abnermal.

"It's not working," reported Garzooka. "The wall is holding. There's no sign of a crack anywhere."

The temperature in the room dropped quickly, and Abnermal's four friends were soon shivering where they stood. Then Garzooka had an idea. "Keep the freeze power going, Abnermal," he ordered. "Maybe the lower temperature has weakened the metal enough that a powerful blow will shatter it."

Garzooka turned to the strongest member of Pet Force: Odious. An icicle of frozen drool hung from his mouth. "Go for it, Odious," said Garzooka. "You are our last hope."

Odious nodded, cracking off the icicle. Then he drew back his enormous fist and let loose with the most powerful punch he had ever thrown.

The room shook from the impact. The other

members of Pet Force were knocked off their feet, but the walls that imprisoned them held solidly.

Abnermal let go of the wall, and the room soon returned to its normal temperature. "Compooky, can you give us an analysis of the metal from which the wall is made?" asked Garzooka.

"Scanning," said Compooky as he flashed and beeped for several seconds. "This is some new type of metal I am not familiar with."

"Vetvix has been busy," hissed Garzooka. "She's obviously come up with a new metal alloy that is impervious to our powers!"

"Huh?" said Abnermal. "Translation, please."

"We can't get out of here," said Garzooka very slowly. *"We are trapped!"*

At that moment, Vetvix's evil laughter filled the metal prison. "Had your fun, Pet Fools?" she sneered. "You are quite right, Garzooka. The walls that now hold you are indeed made of a brand-new type of metal, one I recently invented in my Lethal Lab.

"And yes, I have been extremely busy on a few other projects as well. It was so good of you to walk right into my perfectly planned trap. I gave Pie-Rat instructions to lead you here should you decide to interfere with our tasty little plan for domination of this entire universe.

"You see, I have another surprise for you. In addition to the levitation ray that Pie-Rat has been using to steal food and the unbreakable metal walls that now surround you, I have created my most powerful weapon ever.

"It has taken me years to trap you, but my plan is finally complete. Today is a day that will long be talked about in story and song throughout the universe, for today will see the end of Pet Force!"

"What is she talking about?" snarled Starlena.

"Good question," came Vetvix's reply. "I have developed a weapon that will strip you of your Pet Force powers. And, oh, yes, I almost forgot — this weapon has another nasty little side effect: It will transport you to a ghostly dimension where you will remain forever. You will not be dead, but you will also not be able to communicate with anyone in your own dimension.

"And now I say the words I've been longing to say for years — *Good-bye and good riddance, Pet Force!*"

Before any of the superheroes had a chance to react, the metal box that held them was flooded with a sickly green light the color of cafeteria walls. One by one, the members of Pet Force fell to the ground in pain. They grew weaker and weaker, and then suddenly they vanished. The green light disappeared. The metal prison — which just seconds before had contained the five superpowered beings known as Pet Force — was now empty.

High above, on a landing in the abandoned factory, Vetvix and Space Pie-Rat celebrated.

"That was nice work, Vetvix," Space Pie-Rat complimented her.

Vetvix smiled a satisfied smile. "Now there is nothing to stop me from taking total control of this entire universe! Emperor Jon, your days as ruler are numbered!"

7

Emperor Jon paced back and forth impatiently across his wood-paneled throne room. His plaid sneakers squeaked on the highly polished linoleum floor. *Squeak, squeak, squeak,* turn. *Squeak, squeak, squeak,* turn. *Squeak, squeak, squeak,* turn. On each trip, he paused in front of the giant view screen. Staring at the endless collection of stars, Jon shook his head nervously, then resumed his pacing. *Squeak, squeak, squeak,* turn. And on it went.

It had been several days since his communication with Garzooka. Emperor Jon had spent the entire time locked in his throne room, taking all his meals there and even sleeping on a folding cot in the corner, waiting for some word from Pet Force.

"Garzooka and his team have battled Vetvix many times," said Emperor Jon aloud, trying to calm himself down. "They've always been able to use their great powers and quick wits — well,

most of them — to get out of any trap she could throw their way. So I shouldn't worry, right?

"Wait a minute. Who am I talking to?"

Emperor Jon went back to his pacing.

Suddenly a great commotion erupted in the palace. The emperor heard the sound of people running frantically through the halls. Shrieks filled the air, along with cries of "Emperor Jon!" and "We've got to tell the emperor!"

Emperor Jon grabbed the handle and tried to pull the door to the throne room open. After two or three pulls, he remembered that he had locked himself in so he wouldn't be disturbed. Fumbling for the keys, he unlocked the door and dashed from the throne room.

As he scrambled through the halls of his palace, Emperor Jon ran alongside his subjects and servants. "It's here!" someone called out. "It has returned!" shouted someone else.

Emperor Jon dashed through the sliding patio doors he had substituted for the original oak front doors at the entrance to his palace, bursting out into the bright sunshine of a warm afternoon on the planet Polyester. Making his way to the center of the crowd, the emperor looked up, and his thin jaw dropped open in amazement. There, hovering in the sky above his palace, was the *Lightspeed Lasagna*, Pet Force's spaceship.

Back in his throne room, Emperor Jon resumed his pacing. He stopped and stared at the banquet table with the view screen and computer console, knowing what he had to do, yet putting it off for as long as he could.

Emperor Jon was convinced that something terrible had happened to Pet Force. The *Lightspeed Lasagna* had a homing device programmed to automatically pilot the ship to the emperor's palace on the planet Polyester if no member of Pet Force came aboard for forty-eight hours. The fact that the ship now hovered in the sky above his palace with no sign of any Pet Force members told Jon that something was very wrong.

The *Lightspeed Lasagna* was also equipped with a recording device that kept a video log of everything that happened to Pet Force. A camera attached to one of the members' belts relayed images to the ship.

Emperor Jon sat down at the computer console and downloaded the video log from the *Lightspeed Lasagna*. He took a deep breath, then played back the film.

He watched, horrified, as Pet Force was trapped by Vetvix. He watched their escape attempts, and finally, he watched as the five heroes he had come to trust and rely upon were stripped of all their powers by Vetvix's weapon and sent into the ghostly dimension, lost forever to his universe.

The ship's log ended abruptly. The final image was a blinding flash of light. The final sound was Vetvix's triumphant laugh.

8

Emperor Jon slumped back into his recliner throne. He thought about what he had just seen and shook his head sadly. As it all sank in, he realized he had lost his five friends and faithful warriors. He also realized that his universe, long at peace, was now in grave danger of being taken over by the hateful Vetvix.

He resumed his pacing, his sneakers once again squeaking on the linoleum floor. "I need help," he said aloud. "I can't fight Vetvix's dark magic alone. With Pet Force gone, I need some magic of my own!"

Emperor Jon summoned a well-known sorcerer to his palace. Sorcerer Binky just happened to look very similar to Garfield's favorite television clown in our universe, Binky the Clown. Emperor Jon was seeking advice and some magical help from Sorcerer Binky. He needed something to stop the now-unchecked power of Vetvix.

Sorcerer Binky burst into Emperor Jon's throne

room dragging a large sack behind him. "WHAT IS IT YOU REQUIRE, O GREAT EMPEROR?" he shouted in a voice that sounded like it came from a bullhorn.

"The first thing I require is that you lower your voice a bit," replied Emperor Jon.

"I DID LOWER IT!" said Sorcerer Binky. "DO YOU WANT TO HEAR MY *LOUD* VOICE?"

The force of Sorcerer Binky's voice pinned Emperor Jon against his throne. The headrest and footrest popped out, and Jon found himself in a reclining position. "No. Can you take it down another hundred decibels or so?" he asked, as he resettled himself into a sitting position.

"WHATEVER YOU COMMAND, O GREAT EMPEROR!" replied Sorcerer Binky. With that, he pulled a magic wand from his long black-and-gold robe, flipped it up into the air like a baton, then caught it in his mouth, swallowing the long, thin rod in one gulp.

"There," he said in a normal voice. "That voice-lowering spell should last for a while." The sorcerer adjusted his tall, pointy hat with the pom-pom on top. "Now, what is it that causes you to summon me here to your beautifully decorated throne room?"

Emperor Jon proceeded to tell the sorcerer about Vetvix's plan to control the food supply of the universe. He then told Sorcerer Binky about the fate that had befallen the Pet Force.

"Fear not, O Great Emperor," said Sorcerer Binky. "I have just the thing you need right here in my little black bag." The sorcerer dragged his large sack over to the throne. Untying the string that held it closed, he pulled open the sack to reveal a large black cast-iron cauldron. "One genuine, regulation, magic-type cauldron at your service."

"Wow!" said Emperor Jon, unable to think of anything more clever to say.

"You like it?" asked the sorcerer. "I got it at Cauldrons-Я-Us, on sale. Only four goats and fifteen chickens."

"Sounds like a bargain to me," said the emperor. "What's it do?"

"This baby is fully loaded," the sorcerer told him. "Not only does it make a vegetable soup to die for, but it also can open the doorway between this universe and any one of the infinite number of parallel universes that we know to exist. And that's where I think I can give you a hand.

"You see, the powers of Pet Force are a rare and special gift. Only beings with similar genetic structures to those of the poor departed Pet Force members can receive those Pet Force powers. We need to find a group of five such beings in one of the parallel universes. Understand?"

"I think so," replied the emperor. "You mean we need to find five beings that are sort of *like* Pet Force to *replace* Pet Force. But how do we do it?"

Sorcerer Binky proceeded to fill his cauldron with water, which magically heated up and soon began to boil. To the boiling water the sorcerer added eye of newt, tongue of frog, and a healthy helping of ricotta cheese. He stirred the bubbling mixture for a few minutes, then he allowed the bubbling to stop. The surface of the strange liquid grew still, and an image started to appear.

"I see something!" exclaimed Emperor Jon. "It looks like a thick white cloud."

"That's just a lump of ricotta cheese," explained the sorcerer. "Let me break that up with the big spoon."

A scene began to take shape in the cauldron — fuzzy at first, then slowly coming into sharper focus.

"LOOK THERE!" shouted Sorcerer Binky at ear-splitting volume once again. "The doorway has been opened to a parallel universe, O Great Emperor. The cauldron has revealed five beings capable of becoming Pet Force!"

The image on the surface of the liquid was that of Garfield, Odie, Arlene, Nermal, and Pooky at a backyard barbecue in our universe.

"*Them?*" asked Emperor Jon, as he watched Garfield shove another hot dog into his mouth and Odie drool on his own foot. "You're kidding! You want these ridiculous beings to save my universe? They don't look like they could save a place in line, much less an entire universe!"

"Trust me, O Great Emperor," replied Binky. "This cauldron works wonders!"

"Very well," said the emperor. "But if you ask me, it's quite a stretch!"

"Now that the doorway between universes is open, I can use the magic of the cauldron to bring the five here," said Sorcerer Binky. "And you will witness an amazing transformation."

"Then do so at once," commanded Emperor Jon, wincing at the thought. "Bring those beings before me! Pet Force must be restored!"

9

In Jon's backyard . . .

The barbecue that Emperor Jon and Sorcerer Binky observed from the emperor's palace in their own universe was taking place on a beautiful sunny summer day in our universe on Earth. It was happening a few weeks after the barbecue where Garfield and his friends had first had their discussion about comic books.

On this day, Nermal was bursting with excitement. He came rushing into the backyard waving a copy of *Pet Force* number 100 over his head and yelling, "It's out! It's out! I got it!"

Arlene was pleased to see Nermal so happy about the giant, double-sized, super-spectacular anniversary issue with the embossed, gold foil, 3-D, holographic, glow-in-the-dark cover. Odie came over to find out what all the excitement was about. "You can't slobber on issue number one hundred, Odie," said Nermal. "But you can listen while I read it to everyone!"

Odie nodded his head happily, then settled down to hear the latest adventures of Pet Force.

"Must we be subjected to this every time we have a barbecue?" asked Garfield between bites of his tenth hot dog of the day. Again, Pooky rested against his hind legs.

"*I* want to hear the story, Nermal," said Arlene.

"Hey, issue number one hundred," said Jon, looking up from his grill long enough to notice that Nermal was holding the prized comic book. "I'm dying to know how Pet Force got out of that elevator trap!"

Nermal gave Garfield a dirty look, then began reading aloud. Everyone except Garfield listened intently as Nermal described how the members of Pet Force, bombarded with Vetvix's molecular scrambling ray, felt their bodies starting to tear apart. Garzooka even felt his razor-sharp claw begin to separate from his paw. He stared at his right hand in horror. Then, looking up, he had an idea.

Garzooka spotted the round mirror that is built into the top far corner of every elevator as a security feature. The mirror allows passengers to see the entire elevator car before they step in.

Garzooka leaped up to the ceiling and slashed the mirror from its stem with his razor-sharp right claw. Gathering the other members of Pet Force close to him, Garzooka held up the large round mirror like a shield. Not only did the circular piece of glass protect the superheroes from the molecular scrambling ray, but its reflective surface sent the ray beaming back to its source, overloading the mechanism and causing it to explode. The explosion ripped the elevator apart, allowing Pet Force to race to their ship and escape from the *Orbiting Clinic of Chaos.*

"Wow! Cool!" exclaimed Nermal.

"Like they've never used that device in a comic book?" groaned Garfield, by this time up to his twentieth hot dog. "Let me guess, Arlene. You've never heard it before!"

Before Arlene could respond to the insult, something very strange began to happen. The special embossed, gold foil, 3-D, holographic, glow-in-the-dark cover of issue number 100 of *Pet Force* began to glow — but it was not dark out. Brilliant sunlight poured down, but the cover shone with an eerie light of its own. Nermal was baffled.

"I've never heard of a glow-in-the-*light* cover," he said, scratching his head in confusion.

Jon didn't notice the cover. He was too intent on not burning any hot dogs this time. As he stared at his grill there was a blinding flash, then Garfield, Odie, Nermal, Arlene, and Pooky were sucked right into the cover of issue number 100 of *Pet Force*, disappearing in an instant.

Just as the sorcerer's cauldron was the doorway between universes in the alternate universe, so the special cover of issue number 100 served as the doorway between universes in our universe. Garfield and his friends were on their way to the greatest adventure of their lives!

10

Emperor Jon's universe . . .

Garfield opened his eyes. He felt dizzy. He looked around at what appeared at first to be familiar surroundings: wood paneling on the walls, linoleum tiles on the floor, and a recliner in the center of the room. *I'm in Jon's den!* he thought. *But how did I get here? And why do I feel so weird? I only had twenty hot dogs!*

He glanced to his left. *And there's Jon, in his long, flowing robe with a gold crown on his head.*

Long, flowing robe with a gold crown on his head?

Garfield stood up and stretched. Confused, he reached up to scratch his head, and a huge muscular arm passed in front of his eyes. *Who's the muscle man?* he wondered. Then he realized that the arm was *his.*

He stepped in front of a full-length mirror and saw that he was now standing upright on his two hind legs, a strapping six feet five inches tall. The heavily muscled arms he now flexed over and over were actually his front legs. His formerly furry paunch rippled with muscles, and his entire body was clothed in Garzooka's superhero costume, complete with tights, belt, boots, and cape.

Am I dreaming? he thought. *Because if I am, this is one of my all-time strangest! Maybe I shouldn't have scarfed down that weeks-old lasagna before I had all those hot dogs! I thought that green stuff on the cheese was just spinach!*

One by one, Garfield's companions opened their eyes and looked around. They realized that they were no longer in their own backyard. Even more bizarre was the fact that they were all changed — transformed into beings with bodies and powers not their own.

Nermal dashed to the mirror. Looking himself up and down, he realized he was wearing the costume of the Pet Force superhero known as Abnermal. Then he looked at the others and saw that each of the five now looked just like a member of Pet Force.

"Oh, my gosh!" Nermal said aloud, finally breaking the silence that had come over the stunned group. "The five of us look exactly like Pet Force!"

"Very observant," said a voice behind Nermal.

All five friends spun around and found themselves face-to-face with —

"Binky the Clown?" exclaimed Garfield.

"Binky the Sorcerer, actually, Garzooka," corrected the sorcerer.

"Garzooka?" replied Garfield. "That's not my name."

"And I am Emperor Jon," said the emperor, stepping forward and bowing slightly.

"*Emperor?*" sputtered Garfield, unable to control his laughter. "Jon, an emperor?" he repeated, clutching his chest, doubled up in hysterics.

"I don't see what's so funny," said Emperor Jon, surprised and a bit annoyed at Garfield's reaction.

Garfield was stunned. "And you can hear us *talk* now, too."

Garfield leaned on a chair to steady himself. The sturdy wooden chair shattered from the force of his enormous strength. "Huh?" he said, his jaw dropping open in disbelief. As his mouth opened, a gamma-radiated hairball shot out and melted a hole in the thick stone wall across the throne room.

Odie, transformed into Odious, had also grown in size and strength. He, too, wore a Pet Force costume, he stood upright on his hind legs, and his body rippled with huge muscles. Unfortunately, his brain power had not increased along with his muscle mass, so he didn't notice much difference.

That is, until he licked Garfield with what had become Odious's super-stretchy stun tongue.

When Odie's tongue touched Garfield's face, Garfield's mind went spinning out of control. All logical thought leaped from his brain, and he felt himself in danger of becoming as dumb as Odie was. Using his newfound strength, Garfield pried Odie's tongue from his face, and his mind returned to normal.

Arlene, who had been changed into Starlena, opened her mouth to speak. "What is going on here?" she asked. Out drifted not the voice of Arlene, but Starlena's beautiful siren song. Its hypnotic power gripped everyone in the room — except Garfield, who was immune to its effects. The others all fell into a trance.

Arlene herself was stunned by the strange melodic tune that came out of her mouth each time she tried to speak. Seeing the effect of her voice on the others, she remained silent long enough for everyone to recover.

Nermal, meanwhile, was out of control. As it dawned on him that he had become one of his comic-book heroes, his excitement mixed with his usual ability to irritate now increased to super-hero size, and he ran over and grabbed each of his friends. "Don't you get it?" he shouted as he raced from Garfield to Arlene to Odie, grasping each of them by the shoulders. "Somehow, someway, we've become Pet Force!" But now that he was

Abnermal, his body temperature was absolute zero, and his touch froze his friends into ice statues.

Fortunately, Sorcerer Binky had foreseen this problem and had an antifreeze formula ready to defrost the frozen friends. This same formula also worked wonders in the radiator of the *Lightspeed Lasagna*!

When they had wiped the last few icicles from their eyes, Garfield and Arlene strode up to Emperor Jon and Sorcerer Binky. "You look spiffy in the robe and crown," began Garfield, "and I just love your palace decorating concept. And the muscles — terrific! But can you please tell us exactly what in the name of tuna salad is going on?"

A series of whistles and clicks came from behind Garfield. He whirled around to see Pooky in his Pet Force identity of Compooky, the super-intelligent part-teddy bear, part-computer.

"My analysis of the mathematical and cosmic data available can lead me to only one conclusion," Compooky said as his friends all listened intently. "We have been transported from our universe into one of the infinite number of parallel universes that are known to exist. Apparently some terrible fate has befallen the members of Pet Force in this universe. Because of our similar genetic makeup we have been brought here and given the powers of Pet Force. I believe we are about to become the superhero defenders of this universe."

"Is this true?" asked a stunned Garfield.

"Your clever friend is correct," replied the sorcerer.

"And we are supposed to work for *Emperor* Jon? Doing what? Picking out his hideous outfits?" howled Garfield.

"I've had about enough of this," said a very annoyed emperor as Garfield laughed in his face. "Sorcerer! Surely there must be five other beings — slightly more polite beings — from some other parallel universe we could use?"

The sorcerer took a minute to calm down the emperor, convincing him that these five would do.

"However, it's obvious you will all need some training in order to use these new powers we have bestowed upon you. That is, if you are willing to take on the awesome responsibility of becoming Pet Force."

Nermal leaped onto Garfield's back. "Oh, please! Oh, please! Oh, please! Can we? Come on!" he whined in his most irritating voice. "Can we please take on the awesome responsibility of becoming Pet Force?" Garfield immediately turned into a frozen statue, so he couldn't hear Nermal's continuing pleas.

Sorcerer Binky defrosted Garfield, who turned and gave Nermal a nasty look. Then, after a brief conference with Arlene, Garfield agreed to use the powers given to him to lead the fight for justice. Arlene agreed, as well.

"You may count me in, too," said Pooky.

All eyes turned to Odie, who slobbered his agreement despite not really understanding what was going on.

"I thank you," said Emperor Jon. "And more important, the pets of this universe thank you."

Sorcerer Binky proceeded to lead the five friends through an intensive training session. Each member of the team practiced controlling his or her powers so that they could be used when needed and not just randomly and dangerously.

Garfield fired a gamma-radiated hairball at a target that Binky had set up. It started moving — right toward Pooky's head!

"Duck!" shouted Garfield. Pooky lowered his head just in time, and the hairball melted an ancient suit of armor that stood in the corner of Jon's throne room.

"He's not a duck," said Nermal, tapping Garfield on the shoulder. "He's a teddy bear."

The spot on Garfield's shoulder where Nermal tapped him froze solid, making Garfield's arm unmovable.

Nermal thought this was extremely funny, and despite reprimands from Binky, he froze one of Garfield's legs just to be extra annoying.

As Binky thawed out Garfield, Arlene tried again to control her voice.

"Hello," she said as softly as possible. Everyone in the room fell into a trance. When Binky woke up, he continued to work with her until she finally learned to control her powerful siren song.

Odie practiced firing his stun tongue. The long, stretchy tongue shot from his mouth, missed the target completely, and struck a chair. The chair shook violently, then fell into a pile of toothpicks.

When Garfield had been completely thawed out, Nermal, never grasping the concept that "enough is enough," headed over to annoy his friend again. Garfield simply swatted Nermal across the room with a flick of his superstrong wrist.

Despite nearly killing one another many times over, the five friends soon learned, under Sorcerer Binky's careful guidance, to master their powers. As the sorcerer helped the team control their abilities, Emperor Jon filled them in on the current, desperate situation in his universe. He explained how Vetvix had sent Space Pie-Rat on a food-stealing rampage that threatened to starve the inhabitants of many planets.

Although he had gained Garzooka's super-powered body, Garfield still had the essence of his own brain. Upon hearing of Pie-Rat's fiendish food raids, he grew furious. "Terrorizing a planet's population is one thing. Stealing their *food* is quite another! It's unforgivable! Come on, Arlene, Odie, Nermal, Pooky. Let's go save the universe!"

"It would actually help all of you in controlling your powers if you think of yourselves as Pet

61

Force, rather than as your true identities," explained Sorcerer Binky. "Therefore, I suggest that from now on, you use your Pet Force names at all times."

The five friends nodded in agreement.

"*Garzooka!*" shouted Garfield.

"*Starlena!*"

"*Abnermal!*"

"*Compooky!*"

Slobber! Odious gave an extra-big slobber.

"PET FORCE IS REBORN!" exclaimed Sorcerer Binky, unable to keep his ultra-loud voice under control. "Now take Pet Force's spaceship, the *Lightspeed Lasagna*, and go stop Space Pie-Rat and Vetvix!"

The five reborn members of Pet Force charged from the emperor's throne room, heading for the *Lightspeed Lasagna*. On the way, Abnermal couldn't resist freezing Garzooka's arm just one more time.

11

On board his spaceship, the *Ravenous Rodent*, Space Pie-Rat finished the last bit of a two-gallon tub of ice cream. He tossed the empty container over his shoulder and reached for a large pizza with double cheese piled high with mushrooms. Both items were part of Pie-Rat's hoard of stolen food — the bulk of which he now towed behind the *Ravenous Rodent* in an ever-increasing line of cargo ships.

"Ah," Pie-Rat sighed. "Life is good when you love your work." Then he shoved half of the pizza hungrily into his mouth. "And with that pesky Pet Force out of the way, it's easy, too! Planet after planet filled with food, ripe for the picking."

As Pie-Rat sat feeding his face at the helm of the *Ravenous Rodent*, his army of Vetvix's mutant animals scurried busily around the ship. A moose with an eagle's head came trotting up to Pie-Rat just as he finished the last bite of pizza.

"We're approaching the planet Lox, Captain," reported the moose-eagle. "Our advance spies tell us that at some point next year, its sun will go supernova, but right now it has tons of food — especially breakfast stuff — so it's worth hitting."

"Prepare for landing!" said Pie-Rat through a mouthful of chocolate-chip cookies.

Leaving his caravan of cargo ships in orbit, Space Pie-Rat piloted the *Ravenous Rodent* down to the planet's surface. Once he had landed, he turned loose Vetvix's army of mutant animals.

An elephant with a snake's head spewed a stream of venom powerful enough to paralyze half a city. At the same time, a monkey with a crow's head swung from treetops to building roofs, letting out a piercing shriek that caused people by the hundreds to clutch their ears and pass out.

While his army of mutant animals subdued the population of the planet Lox, Space Pie-Rat was busy setting up his levitation ray. When it was ready, he flipped on the ray and aimed it at a food storage warehouse. The entire warehouse full of food lifted up to a waiting cargo ship in orbit high above the planet's surface.

"This is like taking candy from a baby," Pie-Rat guffawed as he levitated another warehouse of food off the planet. "As a matter of fact, that sounds like a pretty good idea. I should remember to try it sometime."

Space Pie-Rat's glee was suddenly cut short by

the deafening roar of a spaceship engine. A huge shadow appeared overhead.

"What's this?" he yelled. Looking up, he saw the *Lightspeed Lasagna* swooping down for a landing. "But that's impossible!" he cried. "Pet Force was destroyed. I saw it happen with my own one eye!"

The *Lightspeed Lasagna* set down, a hatch slid open, and out burst Pet Force. The five teammates swung into action, shouting, *"Let the fur fly!"*

It had taken Compooky only a few seconds to learn how to pilot the *Lightspeed Lasagna*. Once they were out in space, Pie-Rat's trail was not hard to pick up. Since the destruction of the original Pet Force, Pie-Rat had gotten sloppier than usual. Fearing nothing, he had left a long trail of garbage behind the *Ravenous Rodent* that stretched across the universe.

Pie-Rat now screamed in shock at the sight of the newly reborn heroes. His army of mutants heard the cry and rallied to his side. The part-elephant, part-snake creature fired a stream of paralyzing venom right at Odious!

Abnermal leaped in front of Odious, putting up his invisible energy shield. "Pet Force rules!" shouted Abnermal as the toxic venom splattered against the shield and fell away harmlessly. Odious, dumb as a stump in any universe, didn't realize that he had been saved from a vicious attack. He thought that the elephant-snake creature was just playing. He returned the favor by shooting his super-stretchy stun tongue right at the animal, causing it to suffer total mental meltdown.

Meanwhile, the part-monkey, part-crow beast leaped down from a tree, landing right in front of Starlena. The creature let loose with its eardrum-shattering shriek, which stunned Pet Force for a moment. Starlena fell unconscious to the ground. The monkey-crow quickly jumped on Garzooka's head and shrieked into his ear. Garzooka, too, fell to the ground, unconscious.

Space Pie-Rat then fired his levitation ray at Abnermal and Odious. The two heroes floated in the air, where they hung, helpless. Pet Force was paralyzed.

"All too easy," squealed Pie-Rat. "I thought at least you guys would give me a challenge!"

Starlena slowly returned to consciousness. She opened her eyes and saw Pie-Rat dragging away Garzooka's limp body. *Could we be defeated so easily in our very first battle?* she thought. *Never!* Focusing on what she had learned in her training, Starlena fired a concentrated siren song blast at Pie-Rat.

Her supersonic voice struck the rodent and knocked him off his feet. It also had the unexpected effect of reviving Garzooka and filling him with new energy.

Garzooka leaped to his feet. "Your food-stealing

days are over, you wretched rodent!" he shouted as he raced over to the levitation ray. Revealing his razor-sharp right claw, Garzooka cut through the levitation ray like a slicing machine through a bakery rye bread, destroying the device of destruction. Abnermal and Odious plummeted toward the ground. Garzooka reached out and easily caught one teammate in each hand.

"I *like* this!" exclaimed Garzooka. "Big muscles, a razor-sharp right claw, incredible strength — I could get used to this!"

"Oh, yeah? Well, how about *this*, Lard-zooka?" came a voice from behind Garzooka. Before he could react, Space Pie-Rat had climbed onto his back, knocking the Pet Force leader to the ground. "I don't know how you annoying do-gooders escaped, but right now, you are mine!" shouted the enraged rodent.

"With dialogue like that, it's obvious you've read too many hokey old comic books, Pie-Rat," said Garzooka as he flipped the rodent over onto his back. "Should I make fun of your name, too, and call you 'Space Door-Mat' for comic effect?"

"Not terribly funny, Gar-boob-ka," replied Pie-Rat as Garzooka swung his massive fist. Pie-Rat rolled out of the way just in time. Garzooka's powerful punch smashed a huge hole in the ground.

"Your pathetic taunts are getting worse, Pie-Rat," said Garzooka, dodging a fairly feeble swing.

"And I'm getting tired of this cat-and-mouse game we're playing."

"You mean cat-and-*rat*, don't you?" shot back Pie-Rat.

"I mean to end this battle right here!" shouted Garzooka. He swiped at Pie-Rat with his razor-sharp right claw, slicing off the rodent's eye patch to reveal . . . a perfectly normal eye!

"I just liked the look," admitted Pie-Rat with a shrug.

Garzooka slipped the eye patch into a secret pocket in his cape, keeping it as a memento of his first battle as a superhero. Then, with a sudden, swift blow, Garzooka sent Pie-Rat flying. Unfortunately, the villain landed right at the foot of the *Ravenous Rodent*. Before Pet Force could stop him, Pie-Rat had blasted off, leaving his mutant army and cargo ships behind.

12

Pet Force followed close behind the *Ravenous Rodent* in the *Lightspeed Lasagna*. "Having superpowers is really fun!" exclaimed Abnermal once they were underway. He had mastered his freeze power, and now he walked around the ship freezing and unfreezing chairs, books, food — whatever he could get his hands on. "Did you see me put up my shield to save Odious from that snake creature's venom blast? Did you see, huh? Zap! I was quick as lightning!"

"I think we were all just a little bit busy using our own powers to pay attention to *you*," replied Garzooka. "This is Pet Force, remember? Not the Incredible Abnermal Adventure Hour."

"What a great name for a show!" Abnermal said, taking Garzooka seriously. "We could open each week with —"

"I think Garzooka's point was that we were given these powers to work as a team," interrupted Starlena, "not for individual glory. I, for

one, think we did pretty well for a bunch of pets who have only been superheroes for a few days."

"I agree," added Compooky. "My analysis of our performance in our first true test against a real live enemy indicates that we were operating at eighty-seven percent of maximum efficiency."

"I wonder where that other thirteen percent went?" said Starlena.

At that moment, Odious walked past Starlena licking a spare boot that Abnermal had frozen like a Popsicle.

"Oh," said Starlena, watching Odious. "Never mind."

"So where do you think Space Pie-Rat is headed, huh?" asked Abnermal. "Is he off to raid another planet, giving me a chance to use my incredible superpowers again? Are we going to follow him wherever he goes? What if he goes into a nebula, or a supernova, or a star cluster, or an ion storm, or —"

As Garzooka, Garfield had acquired a lot more patience than he had ever displayed in his own universe. But even superpowered patience has a limit, and Garzooka had just reached his. "It seems to me that your power to irritate outweighs all your other powers," he said. With that, he grabbed Abnermal, lifted him over his head, and pinned him to the ceiling of the ship. "Now go man your station and stop asking so many questions before I use my superpowerful fist to flatten you."

Garzooka tossed Abnermal across the ship, where he landed in his chair. "Now," said Garzooka, as Abnermal mumbled and grumbled and checked out his star charts, "to answer the only important question you asked, I'm sure that Space Pie-Rat is headed to the *Orbiting Clinic of Chaos*, which means that we are on our way to our first confrontation with Vetvix!"

Sure enough, as the *Lightspeed Lasagna* followed the *Ravenous Rodent*, it became clear that they were headed for Vetvix's headquarters, the *Orbiting Clinic of Chaos*. A short time later, the monstrous space station came into view. It loomed before them — a gigantic glass-and-steel office building in space.

"Stay sharp, guys," said Starlena as the tension grew on board the *Lightspeed Lasagna*. "We don't want to get trapped like the original Pet Force."

"Starlena's right," agreed Garzooka. "I'd really rather not end up in that ghostly dimension. I look terrible in white."

Pet Force watched as the *Ravenous Rodent* disappeared into the safety of the *Orbiting Clinic of Chaos*. As soon as Space Pie-Rat's ship was inside the massive space station, Vetvix activated her many weapons systems and opened fire on the *Lightspeed Lasagna*.

"Now you can be useful, Abnermal!" shouted Garzooka as Compooky just barely managed to maneuver out of the way of a laser blast from the station. "See if you can put your shield up around the ship. It's our only chance to get in there in one piece."

Abnermal concentrated with all his might, extending his shield to cover the entire *Lightspeed Lasagna*. Putting forth every ounce of effort he could muster, Abnermal held his shield against Vetvix's attacks.

"We can't just pull into one of the *Clinic*'s docking bays, like the original Pet Force — that led them right into a trap! We need to find another way in," said Garzooka as laser blasts, proton particles, and huge slabs of radioactive luncheon loaf bounced off Abnermal's shield.

Compooky whistled and beeped as he scanned the station, then reported his findings. "My sensors detect an open air vent on the far side of the station, Garzooka. I suggest you permit me to pilot the ship over to the vent, which will allow you four to enter the *Clinic* through the opening."

"Good plan, Compooky," said Garzooka. "How's the shield holding, Abnermal?"

"Fine, thanks," growled Abnermal through tightly clenched teeth. "But some speed would be appreciated!"

"You got it," said Garzooka, hitting the ship's thrusters. "Compooky, take over the piloting controls. Pet Force, get ready to move!"

Compooky steered the *Lightspeed Lasagna*

over to the open air vent. Deactivating the forward thrusters, he brought the ship to a stop.

"On three," ordered Garzooka. "One, two, *go!*"

"Go?" said Abnermal, still straining to maintain his shield. "What about three?"

"All right," groaned Garzooka. "*Three!*"

Abnermal released his shield just as Compooky opened a hatch in the bottom of the ship. Garzooka, Abnermal, Starlena, and Odious leaped out of the ship and into the air vent. Compooky remained on board.

"We're in!" shouted Garzooka as the four Pet Force teammates landed inside the *Clinic*.

"But," said Starlena urgently, "we're not alone!"

A squadron of Vetvix's mutant animals charged at Pet Force. Garzooka pounded furiously with his fabulous fists, bashing his way through the mass of monstrous mutants. He fired gamma-radiated hairballs as he battled, taking out mutants at long range while he smashed those closer at hand.

Abnermal, although weakened from his effort at maintaining his shield, took great delight in freezing every mutant he could touch. Meanwhile, Odious imitated Garzooka and put his great strength to work pounding mutants with his huge fists. He stunned others with his super-stretchy stun tongue.

Pet Force battled their way deeper and deeper into the *Clinic*. The mutant animals that got past

Garzooka, Odious, and Abnermal were placed into a hypnotic trance and rendered quite harmless by Starlena's siren song.

At the center of the space station, Pet Force came to a large steel door. "I'll bet Vetvix is in this room," said Abnermal. "Let's go!"

"No, wait!" shouted Garzooka. But it was too late. Pet Force followed Abnermal into the room, which turned out to be Vetvix's Waiting Room of Doom. The carpeted, paneled room was lined with uncomfortable chairs and piled high with stacks and stacks of terribly out-of-date magazines.

The stacks of magazines seemed to grow larger as Pet Force watched. Then Starlena realized that the room was filling up with the magazines, threatening to suffocate the heroes. "This must be one of Vetvix's spells!" she cried.

Each of the heroes grabbed at the magazines, which now came flying at them from all directions. "*Better Homes and Litter Boxes*, October 1978!" exclaimed Garzooka, looking at the cover of a magazine he had managed to grasp as it flew past his head.

"*Mewsweek*, January 1965!" cried Starlena.

"*Mouse Beautiful*, July 1980," read Abnermal.

Odious held a copy of *Dogs' Life* in his mouth and shook it violently. Hundreds of subscription cards came flying out, adding to the growing mountain of paper that was burying Pet Force alive.

Garzooka had to think fast. Unfurling his razor-sharp right claw, he began slicing and slashing until all the magazines in the room had been shredded into confetti. He then moved to the door between the waiting room and the office — Vetvix's inner sanctum, her Lethal Lab!

"Next!" shouted Garzooka as he smashed open the door and led his teammates from the Waiting Room of Doom into the Lethal Lab. There they found themselves face-to-face with Vetvix!

13

When he landed at the *Orbiting Clinic of Chaos*, Space Pie-Rat had told Vetvix of his encounter with Pet Force. She didn't believe that the five heroes could really be alive, here in this universe, after she had transported them to the ghostly dimension. She was furious with Pie-Rat for leaving his huge cargo of stolen food behind. But now, with the four heroes standing before her, she had no choice but to believe him.

"So, Pie-Rat, you were telling me the truth," she screamed at her battered henchman. "You incompetent fool. You have failed me for the last time!"

"Sheesh!" said Garzooka. "And I thought *Pie-Rat* read too many hokey old comic books!"

"You were never anything but a weak little mouse, Pie-Rat," snarled Vetvix, still enraged at her henchman's failure. "And so, that's exactly what you'll be!" She closed her eyes and waved her arms in a strange pattern. The power crystal on her headband began to glow, and an evil spell surrounded Space Pie-Rat.

A blinding flash filled the room. When it was gone, Space Pie-Rat had been transformed into a tiny white mouse. The small, frightened creature squeaked and scampered across the floor of the Lethal Lab.

Starlena took advantage of Vetvix's distraction and let loose with her siren song to try to catch the evil veterinarian by surprise. But Vetvix projected a force shield from the crystal in her headband to block the hypnotic power of the song. "Nice try, Madonna," shrieked Vetvix, "but no hit record this time!"

"I think her tune is really hot," Abnermal quipped, "so why don't you just cool down?" He fired a freeze blast that shattered Vetvix's shield.

Before Starlena could release another siren song, Vetvix pulled out her genetic disassembler ray — the very weapon she had used to strip the original Pet Force of their powers and send them to the ghostly dimension.

"Once again," she chortled as she turned on the weapon and fired it at the heroes, "I get to say — *Good-bye and good riddance, Pet Force!*"

This time, nothing happened.

"*Nooooo!*" screamed an enraged Vetvix. "How can my greatness and scientific genius possibly have failed? How many times do I have to destroy you, Pet Creeps?" With a horrific cry, Vetvix smashed her weapon to the floor, shattering it into pieces. "Stupid ray. It must only work on beings the first time they're exposed to it. But don't worry. I have other tricks up my dark sleeve!"

She stumbled to a computer console and set a program into motion. "This time, Pet Force, there is no escape . . . for you, that is!" Closing her eyes and clenching her fists, Vetvix disappeared in a thick green cloud of smoke.

"What did she mean, 'no escape'?" Abnermal asked as the four heroes moved to the computer console.

On a small screen, a countdown was underway. The numbers flashed . . . *30* . . . *29* . . . *28* . . . Garzooka used the Lethal Lab's radio system to make contact with Compooky on board the *Lightspeed Lasagna*. "Can you analyze this computer countdown and tell us what it means?" asked the Pet Force leader.

Garzooka heard Compooky's familiar beeps and whistles. "Vetvix has set an explosive device to go off in thirty seconds — well, twenty-four seconds now — that will blow up the entire *Orbiting Clinic of Chaos*!"

"Can you disarm it?" asked Garzooka.

"I'm afraid not," replied Compooky. "Vetvix has set some kind of security code. It would take me at least a few minutes to break the code."

"We'll meet you back at the air vent, then. You can pick us up there," said Garzooka, panic just beginning to show in his voice as the countdown continued :

19 . . . 18 . . . 17 . . .

"We'll never make it in time," said Starlena. "It would take us at least five minutes to get back to the air vent."

"Is there any other way out of here?" asked Garzooka, trying to remain calm with thirteen seconds left before the *Clinic* exploded.

"The transmitting tower attached to the radio system you are using now is directly above you," explained Compooky. "I will be waiting there. I suggest you hurry!"

"Thanks for the suggestion," said Garzooka as he led the others from the lab. "It doesn't take a superintelligent computer to figure that one out!"

Pet Force clambered up a circular metal staircase. Sliding open a narrow rectangular doorway, the four heroes squeezed through the opening and pulled themselves onto the roof of the *Clinic*.

A tall transmitting tower extended straight up from the roof. The *Lightspeed Lasagna* hovered at the top of the tower with its bottom hatchway open. One by one the members of Pet Force scrambled up the tower and climbed on board the ship.

"Get us out of here, Compooky!" Garzooka shouted when all the members of Pet Force were aboard. Compooky hit the main thrusters, and the *Lightspeed Lasagna* shot away from the *Orbiting*

Clinic of Chaos just as the *Clinic* exploded in a fiery blast of orange and red.

"Nice work, Pet Force," said Garzooka, who had come to enjoy the whole superhero business in this universe. He looked over at Odious, who was playing with something.

"What's that?" asked Starlena.

Odious picked up the tiny object and carried it over to Starlena. He dropped it in front of her, and it scurried across the floor of the ship.

"It's Pie-Rat in his mousy form!" exclaimed Starlena, laughing. "You took him with you!"

Odious again grabbed the tiny white mouse delicately as the rest of the crew laughed.

The *Lightspeed Lasagna* returned to the planet Polyester. The five members of Pet Force were soon in the throne room of Emperor Jon's castle, standing before the emperor and Sorcerer Binky.

"Congratulations, Pet Force," said the emperor, after he had heard the details of their successful mission. "A job well done." Then his tone turned serious. "But knowing Vetvix," he added, "she'll definitely be back. We may once again need your services as Pet Force. For now I believe Sorcerer Binky can return you to your own universe. Know that you take my thanks with you."

"No problem," said Garzooka. "And by the way, we have something for you. Odious?"

Odious walked over and dropped the tiny mouse into Emperor Jon's lap. "Space Pie-Rat," said the emperor. "I definitely like the new look." He placed the mouse in a small cage, then turned back to Pet Force. "Farewell, my friends. We will meet again, I'm sure. Binky?"

"All right, I want each of you to close your eyes," Binky began, "click your heels together three times, and say, 'There's no place like my own universe' over and over."

"That's really weird," said Garzooka. "Where'd you come up with that one?"

"Oh, forget it," the sorcerer decided. "That's the old-fashioned way. I've got the advantage of modern magical science at my disposal. Have a nice trip!" Then he reached into his pocket, pulled out a few pellets, dropped them into his bubbling cauldron, and *poof!* Pet Force disappeared.

14

Back in Jon's backyard . . .

Garfield, Odie, Arlene, Nermal, and Pooky reemerged through the cover of *Pet Force* issue number 100, back in their own universe. They were once again in their nonsuperhero forms. They arrived in the backyard just as Jon looked up from checking on the hot dogs on the grill. He had never even noticed that they were gone. Their entire adventure in the alternate universe had happened in the time it took Jon to look down at his grill, then look back up again.

"Who's ready for another hot dog?" asked Jon.

Garfield turned to his friends. "Did I just have a bad dream from eating too many hot dogs?" he asked.

"Well, if you did, I did, too," replied Arlene.

"Did we really go through the cover of *Pet Force* issue number one hundred and become Pet Force in the other universe?" asked Nermal.

85

"Because if we did, that was the coolest thing that ever happened to me!"

"Not tripping over your own feet could qualify as the coolest thing that ever happened to you," replied Garfield, starting to feel more like his old self.

"But if it didn't really happen," Arlene said, "how did we all experience the same dream?"

"Don't tell me nobody wants another hot dog!" exclaimed Jon in shock.

Garfield snapped back to his senses. He reached up and grabbed five hot dogs from Jon, then settled back down to eat and think.

That evening, as an exhausted Garfield stretched out for a good night's sleep, he felt something in his fur that was making him uncomfortable. He reached down and pulled out the black eye patch he had taken from Space Pie-Rat during their battle!

Now he knew his adventure had been real! There were only two questions remaining: Would it ever happen again? And what time was Jon serving breakfast tomorrow morning?